Children's Books:
The Very Helpful Monsters

Sally Huss

ISBN: 0692351809
ISBN 13: 9780692351802

"I want to be a monster," announced Herbie, a very little fellow. "I want to be a monster with all my heart."

Herbie was serious about his desire. He knew what he wanted and he was willing to work for it. But how was he going to be a monster if he didn't know how?

Aha, he thought, he would go to monster school.

Surely there must be a school to teach those who wanted to be monsters how to become one.

So he did what any young lad would do, he checked out the Internet. A Google search would help him find one, he was sure.

Monster schools!

Monster schools!

There were minister schools, manager schools, mortgage schools, music schools, medical schools, but no monster schools.

No problem, thought Herbie, he would take another tack. There would certainly be books on Amazon on how to become a monster.

Again, there were books on how to cook, how to write, how to paint, how to play tennis, how to lose weight, how to gain weight, even how to be happy. But again, there were no books on how to become a monster.

Hmmmm. He thought some more. Aha, one of the best ways to learn something is to ask a professional. In this case, it would be from a monster himself.

Yes, that's what he would do -- ask a monster.

Now the only thing Herbie knew about monsters was that they liked dark places, like under beds.

So one night, after crawling in bed to go to sleep, he crawled out of bed and took a peek.

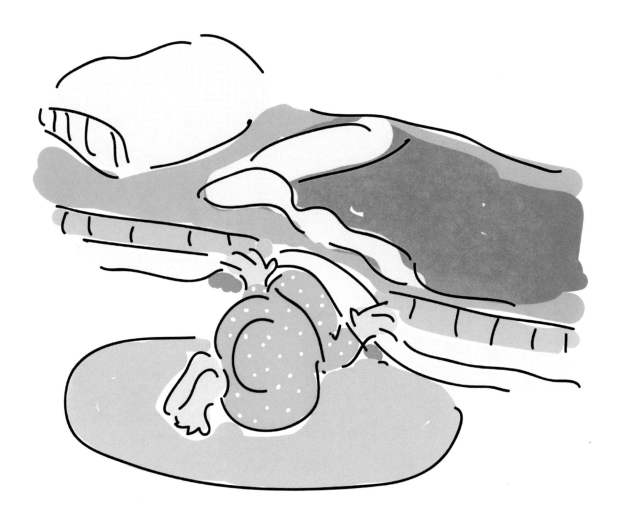

He stuck his head under his bed and hoped for the best, which was hoping for the worst, a monster.

Then, POW! BANG! SPLAT! SQUASH! ERK! Out of the dark a monster appeared.

He yelled and screamed at Herbie in the worst way…
Herbie just smiled.

The monster was taken aback, "Why are you smiling? Why aren't you scared?"

Herbie apologized, "I'm sorry. I just wanted to meet you."

"This is no good. I'm a monster. I scare people; that's what I do. If I don't scare people, I'm not a very good monster."

Then he collected himself, "Why did you want to meet me?"

"I want to be a monster myself."

"Why would you want to do that?" the monster asked.

"You see, I'm very small," explained Herbie, "and I want people to notice me. If I'm a monster, for sure they'll notice me."

"Oh well, in that case you'll have to start by improving your looks. You're too clean. Here put some of these old dust balls all over you."

"Thanks," said Herbie, trying to fasten the dust balls to himself as best he could.

"And try to look scary, then you might want to go see the monster in the closet and ask him what he thinks you should do."

With that Herbie, who was now covered in dust balls, headed to the closet.

He carefully opened the door, stuck his head in and got a frightful reception.

ZING! ZAT! MORENG! DING! FRENG! STOMP! A dark and ferocious monster showed his face.

"What are you doing here?" the monster in the closet wanted to know.

Herbie just smiled.

"And why aren't you scared?" the monster asked.

"Oh, I didn't come here to be scared," Herbie explained. "I came to learn how to scare. I want to be a monster myself."

"Why do you want to do that?" the monster asked.

Herbie told the monster what he had told the last one, "I'm very little and I want to make an impression on people. Being a monster is the best way to do that, I believe."

"I see. I see. Well, you're going to need a lot more than a few dust balls to do it. Here have some spider webs," he said, as he hung webs all over Herbie, as if he were decorating a Christmas tree. "And try to look scary."

"Anything else?" Herbie asked.

"Why don't you go visit the monster in the bathroom cupboard?"

"Thanks," said Herbie, So off he went, with dust balls and spider webs dangling about, to visit the monster in the bathroom.

Gingerly Herbie pulled open the cupboard door…

… And WHAM! BAM! POW! PANG! PLATT! SPLATT!

Out jumped monster number three.

Herbie smiled with delight.

"What are you doing here and why aren't you scared?" asked the monster. "I need for you to be scared. I'm not a real monster unless you're scared."

"Sorry." said Herbie, "But I've come for your help. I want to become a monster like you.

"Why would you want to do that?" the monster asked.

"I'm very small," Herbie said again, "and I want to make an impact on others."

"Well, you're surely not going to do that with a few lousy dust balls and some harmless spider webs. Here, have some dark, dingy bathroom mold. That'll take you down a notch or two."

After attaching wads of mold, Herbie thanked monster number three and asked for any suggestions he might have.

"First, wipe that smile off of your face, try to look scary... and go see the monster in the kitchen under the sink."

"Thanks," said Herbie politely and off he jangled into the kitchen for more instruction.

No sooner had Herbie put his head under the sink than…

WHAM! WHACK! GLINKO! CLANG! GRIFFER! GRUMP! GROOP!

And the most frightening face of all appeared in the dark.

Tickled pink, Herbie greeted the monster with giggles.

"Stop that right now! What are you doing here and why aren't you scared?"

"I've come to get your advice on how to become a monster. I want to be a monster with all my heart."

"Then, stop smiling!" the monster ordered. "You'll never be a monster if you keep that up."

"Yes, sir. I'll do the best I can," answered Herbie. "Got any other suggestions for me?"

"You'll need some more frills than a few dust balls, spider webs, and mold. You need some rotten food. Grab some of those orange rinds and banana peels, and some of those egg shells. Stick them on yourself. They'll add a real stench."

"Thank you. Thank you," Herbie said, beneath the garbage he was putting on.

"By the way, why do you want to be a monster?" monster four asked.

"I'm very little and I want others to take note of me. Have you got any other ideas for me?"

"Go see the monster in the cookie jar, and try not to smile."

"Yes, sir," said Herbie, as he crawled from beneath the sink and climbed up on the counter where the cookie jar stood.

Once there, he delicately removed the top of the jar and…

… Out jumped…

… The grumpiest, lumpiest, crankiest, nastiest monster of all!
SPLABO! JABBO! GLABBO! NAPTUCK! MAPRUK! AAAAH!

Herbie was beside himself with delight -- a monster in a cookie jar! Who would have thought of that?

"What are you doing here?" the monster demanded. "And why are you smiling?"

"I'm here to get your advice on how to become a monster. You see I'm very little and I want people to notice me."

"I hate to tell you this, kid, but you're not cut out for it. Monsters only exist if you're afraid of them."

Every time you would look in the mirror you would see a happy face and the monster in you would disappear. It's nicer to be nice than it is to be mean. You'll make a better impression on others that way than by trying to scare them."

There was disappointment in Herbie's eyes, but he continued to listen to the cookie jar monster.

"Here, have a cookie," said the monster. And with that kind gesture of handing Herbie the cookie, the monster began to grow weaker.

"When the wish to scare others disappears, kindness takes its place," he said as he continued to fade away. "See what I mean?"

At that moment Herbie decided what he would be. He would be a monster all right, but a kind monster and he'd be that with all his heart.

From then on Herbie began to grow. With each bit of kindness that he offered others he became a bigger person. And although he hardly noticed it himself, everyone now noticed him.

The end,
but not the end
of being kind.

At the end of this book you will find a Certificate of Merit that may be issued to any child who honors the requirements stated in the Certificate. This fine Certificate will easily fit into a 5"x7" frame, and happily suit any child who receives it!

Here is another fun book by Sally Huss, all in rhyme.

Synopsis: When a loon, a baboon, and a raccoon complain that they are too close to each other, they move apart. But then they seem to be invading the territory of the local cows, who in turn find them too close. The three move away again, this time to a pond with a school of boorish Moorish idols who are also unwelcoming. They find relief on an island, but that too has inhabitants who insist that they move on. So it goes until the three are surprised by a butterfly who changes their thinking. Perhaps getting along with each other might just be – Cool!

All in rhyme and accompanied by over 25 delightfully colorful illustrations that dance along with the story.

GETTING ALONG WITH EACH OTHER may be found on Amazon as an e-book or soft-cover book -- http://amzn.com/B00JPV4W90.

If you liked THE VERY HELPFUL MONSTERS, please be kind enough to post a short review on Amazon -- http://amzn.com/B00IDSNR7E. Thank you.

If you wish to receive information about upcoming FREE e-book promotions and download a free Sally Huss e-book, go to: http://www.sallyhuss.com.

More Sally Huss books may be viewed on the Author's Profile on Amazon. Here is that URL: http://amzn.to/VpR7B8.

About the Author/Illustrator

Sally Huss

"Bright and happy," "light and whimsical" have been the catch phrases attached to the writings and art of Sally Huss for over 30 years. Sweet images dance across all of Sally's creations, whether in the form of children's books, paintings, wallpaper, ceramics, baby bibs, purses, clothing, or her King Features syndicated newspaper panel "Happy Musings."

Sally creates children's books to uplift the lives of children and hopes you will join her in this effort by helping spread her happy messages.

Sally is a graduate of USC with a degree in Fine Art and through the years has had 26 of her own licensed art galleries throughout the world.

This certificate may be cut out, framed, and presented to any child who has demonstrated her or his worthiness to receive it.

Certificate of Merit

(Name)

The child named above is awarded this Certificate of Merit for practicing kindness every day:

*At home and at school
*With friends
*With siblings
*With everyone

Presented by: _____

Date: _____

Made in the USA
Middletown, DE
28 May 2017